The
Silver Arrow

young Robin Hood
and
the
silver Arrow

RICHARD PERCY

MADCAP

To Dad
With love

First published in Great Britain in 1999
by Madcap Books,
André Deutsch Ltd,
76 Dean Street,
London, W1V 5HA

www.vci.co.uk

Text copyright © 1999 Madcap Books/
Richard Percy

A catalogue record for this title is available from the
British Library

ISBN 0 233 99516 1

Typeset by Derek Doyle & Associates,
Mold, Flintshire
Printed by Mackays of Chatham plc

contents

clarence's problem

Today was the day Robin Hood had been looking forward to for some time. The sun shone brightly over the secret camp in Sherwood Forest and the young fourteen-year-old lay happily in the grass, thinking back over the past two months of living there.

Today they'd decided to make a visit back to their home village of Edwinstowe. He and several of the older ones could travel there and back in a day and pick up food and other supplies. Most importantly, they would see their mothers and pass on news of the younger children.

He watched them now as they played happily on the huge fallen tree which lay across the clearing. Michael, one of his outlaws, had cleverly added slides, swings, pulleys and ropes to the tree, turning it into a wonderful adventure playground.

Robin smiled as he watched them. These were dangerous times. It was important that they could spend their time happily while hidden away in the secret camp.

'What are you smiling at?' Little John's tall figure loomed over him, blocking out the sunlight. Then he folded his long legs and sat down beside Robin.

'I was just counting our blessings,' said Robin. 'We were lucky to find this place, large enough to accommodate thirty-five of us and so well-hidden.' He waved his arms to indicate the clearing surrounded by thick forest on three sides and a huge fallen tree trunk on the other. The only entry to the camp was through a carefully covered hole running under the fallen trunk.

There was no shortage of food either. Fish were caught in the river and nuts and berries gathered from the surrounding forest and Robin and Catherine, the best archers in the camp, took it in turns to sneak out with a bow and arrow and catch rabbits for stew. Michael, being the miller's son, was growing a crop of wheat and he baked delicious loaves of bread every day with grain from the village.

'This is like a little world all on its own,' he

said, 'and so far we have beaten the Sheriff and his evil and unfair laws.'

Little John nodded. They certainly had been lucky. Just two months ago the villagers' lives had changed when they received news of good King Richard. He had been taken prisoner in Vienna and could only be released if twenty loyal men travelled to rescue him. The men of Edwinstowe had bravely decided to make the trip. Their mission was to pay the King's ransom of one thousand gold sovereigns, which they hoped to gain on the long journey to Vienna. If they failed, they must give up their own freedom in exchange for that of the King. Recent news from the men had been optimistic and raised everyone's spirits.

But Robin had had the idea of setting up this camp to keep the children safe and out of the way of the cruel Sheriff of Nottingham, a friend of the wicked Prince John, who was the brother of the king, and who had taken over the throne of England. At least the Sheriff would not be able to use threats against the children to scare the women of Edwinstowe.

'Are the others ready to go?' asked Robin, getting to his feet.

Little John stood up too. 'Anna and Marian are staying behind to look after the younger children,' he said. 'The others are ready. It will be good to get away from the camp for a while.'

None of them had gone very far recently. The Sheriff's men had been searching all over the forest for them for the past two weeks, since Robin and Michael had been rescued from Nottingham Castle. The Sheriff was furious. Robin and his outlaws were becoming famous for stopping the Sheriff doing what he wanted. Everywhere people were saying,

'Robin Hood, he steals from the rich and gives to the poor!'

Before the Sheriff caught them, they had managed to steal a huge treasure chest filled with the valuables belonging to local people, which the Sheriff's men had taken as taxes.

From lookout points all round the camp, the outlaws had watched the Sheriff's search parties and Robin was relieved that they seemed to have died down. The Sheriff had given up, for the moment at least.

Five outlaws, gathered at the fallen tree ready to leave. Robin, Little John, Michael, Catherine and Friar Tuck in his priest's robes.

He was a novice monk with a talent for keeping everyone cheerful.

Robin waved to the children and last of all met Marian's gaze.

'Take care,' she said. 'Come back safely to us.'

He smiled affectionately at her. She was a beautiful maid from Trenton, a neighbouring village to Edwinstowe. Some weeks ago he and his outlaws had rescued her from a marriage to the wicked Sheriff. She was naturally grateful, but he sensed something more in her clear eyes as she held his gaze.

Then with a wave of his hand, he turned to join the others as they crawled through the hole under the log.

The lookouts had given the all-clear and they began their journey along the forest path to Edwinstowe. How pleased their mothers would be to see them.

The journey was uneventful. Although they listened carefully for the sounds of people on the path, they saw nobody and at last, after two hours, they arrived at the edge of the village.

Robin held up his hand for everyone to stop while he crept forward to make sure the Sheriff's men were not in Edwinstowe. When he was certain, he nodded to the others to follow.

'Boo!' called Robin loudly as they entered the kitchen of the manor house. Lizzie, the young kitchen maid, dropped a plate on to the floor where it smashed to pieces.

'Robin! Why must you always startle me?' she scolded him. But as she said it she laughed and wrapped her arms around him. Others had heard the crash and the laughter and soon the kitchen was full of mothers all hugging them and begging for news of their own children.

Lizzie, as usual, began to prepare a meal and Robin and Little John dragged the big table and chairs outside into the courtyard. A cloth was thrown on the table and wooden plates set out and soon the outlaws were tucking into Lizzie's delicious stew.

'My goodness!' declared Mistress Diana Hood, Robin's mother, 'You look as though you haven't eaten for a week! Are you getting enough to eat?'

Robin laughed. 'The walk has made us hungry,' he said between mouthfuls. 'We haven't done so much exercise for a long time as we've been confined to camp.'

Diana looked serious. 'The Sheriff's men have been here nearly every day for the past two weeks asking questions but as we don't know where you are, we can't be forced to tell.'

'Is there any news of the men?' asked Little John, wiping his mouth with his kerchief and looking round the women expectantly.

They shook their heads miserably.

'But we're hopeful,' said Diana, 'since Old Alfred's dream.'

'Tell us,' said Catherine.

'Well, two nights ago,' began Diana, 'he dreamt that he saw them all safe and well in Paris. He says he spoke to your father, Robin, and found out that they had already gathered five hundred gold sovereigns. Before he could ask your father where the coins had come from the dream faded. We pray that his dream was true. It would be wonderful if they were indeed safe and well and making such good progress.'

Everybody sat in silence for a few moments. Alfred's extraordinary powers were well-known. It was he who had verified the truth of the capture of King Richard.

'How about some of your famous fruit cake,

9

Lizzie?' shouted Little John, partly to break the silence and partly because it really was delicious cake.

Nobody spoke for a few moments and Little John looked round, his eyebrows raised questioningly.

'Of course, you've not heard,' said Diana Hood. 'Clarence's fruit crops have been stolen. We have had no fruit from him for the past three weeks.'

They all knew Clarence well. Several years before, his father, the Lord of the Manor, had left him in charge of the estate while he went to fight in the Crusades. Since his father hadn't returned, it was assumed that he must be dead, although Clarence did not accept this.

Clarence had only been seventeen when he had assumed the responsibility of the estate and he had always struggled to do as well as his father. Nobody would have described him as clever, nor was he particularly impressive to look at. He was very thin and bent slightly as he walked. For years he had been a regular visitor to Edwinstowe, where he was well-liked and known to be honest and fair in his selling of fruit to them.

Robin and his friends looked at each other. The Sheriff was still pursuing his evil ways.

'The Sheriff's men took all he had,' went on Diana. 'And told Clarence that they would be back for his main crop, too.'

'Then he won't have any choice but to sell his land to the Sheriff,' said Little John. 'Which is exactly what he's always been after!'

'That's awful,' said Robin.

'Yes,' said his mother. 'But what can anyone do about it? No one can argue with the Sheriff's orders.'

Robin said nothing but mopped up his gravy with a piece of bread, deep in thought. Then he stood up.

'We cannot stay as long as usual. Let's get our supplies and be off.'

Catherine frowned. 'What's the hurry, Robin? We haven't been home for ages. I don't see why we must rush off.'

Robin didn't answer but began gathering up the bundles of food which the women had prepared. The others knew better than to question his actions and it wasn't until they had waved goodbye to the women and were on the path back to the camp that Friar Tuck spoke.

'We'll be home long before nightfall, you know, Robin.'

'I don't think so,' said Robin. 'Not since we have an extra journey to make! We are going to visit Clarence. Somebody has to help him with his problem and that's what we vowed to do, isn't it?'

the old ice pit

2

An hour later Robin and the others arrived at Clarence's estate. They were shocked to see how sad and desperate the poor man looked. He was sitting on a tree stump at the edge of his fields, holding his head in his hands.

Robin walked up and patted him on the shoulder and Clarence turned and looked up at him and then at the others.

'Oh, thank goodness it's you,' said Clarence. 'I thought it may have been the Sheriff's men. I'm expecting them back any day now.'

'Yes,' replied Robin. 'My mother told me that he was up to something. Tell us exactly what's going on. You never know, we may be able to help.'

'I doubt anybody can help,' Clarence said, almost sobbing as he spoke. 'It started three weeks ago, just as I and my two farmers were about to bring the fruit crops in. Suddenly, six of the Sheriff's toughest men appeared saying that they were here to "help" bring in the harvest. In return, I was to give them three-quarters of the crop.'

Robin's lips tightened with anger and he looked at the others, shaking his head. Then they all sat down next to Clarence.

'I couldn't argue,' said Clarence, looking from one to the other. 'They were very threatening.'

'And did they help?' asked Friar Tuck, straightening his brown robes around his feet.

'Hah!' laughed Clarence, mockingly. 'Their idea of helping was to sit outside the barn playing cards all day. The only time they moved was when all the fruit was collected. Then they went into the barn and took three-quarters of the fruit away.'

'And they said they were coming back?' asked Michael.

Clarence nodded. 'They said they would be back in three week's time when the wheat harvest was due. I'm sure they will be here by tomorrow and if I lose the wheat, I'll have no choice but to raise money by selling some land – and there's only one person who will buy it.'

'The Sheriff,' said Little John. 'And he will give you far less than it's worth.'

Clarence nodded miserably.

'Don't despair,' said Little John. 'We're outlaws who steal from the rich and give to the poor. Robin always finds a way to help his friends.'

Robin glared at his friend. It was all very well of Little John to promise to help but without a good plan it was hopeless.

'Would you mind showing us your land?' asked Little John. 'It may just help us to think of something.'

Clarence shrugged his shoulders and stood up. 'I can't think how you could possibly help me but it's kind of you to suggest it.'

He set off across the fields with Robin, Little John, Michael, Friar Tuck and Catherine and seemed to cheer up a little as they walked. The sun was shining. Perhaps there would be a way of outwitting the Sheriff once again.

Robin watched Little John striding ahead, chatting to Clarence. He insisted that they be shown every detail of the fields and then spent a long time studying the wooden barn where the crops would be stored. Finally, he took a great interest in the old ice pit which served the manor house. It was a large hole, almost as big as the manor itself and as deep as a fully-grown man. In winter it was packed with ice and used to keep food fresh. Now, in the middle of summer, it was bare and dry.

At last the tour was finished.

'I've enjoyed showing you round the farm,' said Clarence. 'It's a pleasure to see people take such an interest in it, but it makes me sad to realise just how much I shall be losing. It has been in the hands of my family for generations. What will my father say when he returns? I only wish there was something that could be done.'

To everyone's surprise, Little John spoke up quietly.

'I have a feeling that the answer may be in your own ice pit!' he said. 'In fact, it might be just the ideal place for a brand new barn!'

They all looked at him in amazement.

'What is your plan, Little John?' asked Robin, beginning to feel a bit more optimistic, and as Little John explained it, Robin became more convinced that they might yet again outwit the Sheriff.

It took Clarence a little while before he completely understood what Little John was suggesting, but at last he nodded excitedly and slapped Little John on the back. Then he turned to Robin.

'Do you think it could work, Robin?'

Robin saw the hope shining in his eyes. His plain features had become radiant.

'I think it can work,' said Robin. 'But one thing is for sure. We'll need to work all through the night to get things ready – and we'll need to have plenty of helpers tomorrow.'

He turned to Michael. 'Will you go and fetch Marian, young William and three of the other children from the camp? Tell Anna we shall be away until late tomorrow. I'm sure she will be able to cope.'

When Michael had left, Little John took charge. Under his instruction tools were fetched and the four of them, plus Clarence and his two farmers, began work on the old barn. Carefully they cut away the beams which held it in place. After a little more effort and plenty of pulling and shoving, one end of the barn had been worked loose. It was a start, but there was a lot more still work to be done.

Robin prayed that Little John's plan could really work. If it did, it would be a race against time to get finished before morning, when the Sheriff's men would probably arrive. The plan depended on this because it was essential that the soldiers didn't have any idea of what they had done.

The barn had to be taken down piece by piece and rebuilt just next to where it had originally stood. But this time there would be one major difference. Right in the centre of where the barn now stood would be the old ice pit. And nobody looking inside the barn would know this because new floorboards and sawdust would cover the pit from view!

The soldiers must not notice anything unusual when they arrived. They mustn't be able to tell that the barn had previously stood in a different place or that the floor concealed the ice pit. Only then did the plan have a chance.

the Harvest is hidden

Robin gazed round at the others lying fast asleep in the fields. It was dawn and they had at last finished their long night's work. He too was tired but could not sleep. He looked gratefully at the still forms of Little John, Friar Tuck, Marian, Michael, Catherine and three of the younger children. They had done well and were all exhausted.

Taking the old barn apart had been a huge undertaking and putting it back together again on its new site had been even harder work. Fortunately there had been a full moon.

But now it was done. The ground where the old barn had previously stood had been cleared. If you looked carefully you could see a few marks on the ground where the walls had been but they would just have to hope that the Sheriff's men would not be suspicious enough to examine the ground that closely.

Clarence and his farmers had thanked them all before going to their beds. Now Robin lay back and closed his eyes. He would feel refreshed if he could just have a little sleep...

But it seemed no more than a few minutes later when young William raised the alarm. Three loud cockerel calls was the danger signal that all the outlaws recognised and this time everybody knew what the danger was likely to be.

Robin half sat up and looked through tired eyes in the direction William pointed. He could make out the figures of several men on horseback. In a flash he was on his feet with the others and racing towards the manor house.

'It is well that they are strangers to us,' said Robin, watching the soldiers' approach from a window. 'These men will not recognise us.'

Their leader was a tall man with a brown beard and dressed all in black. As they watched, they saw a smile cross his cruel mouth as he looked across the fields of golden wheat. No doubt he was thinking about the nice bonus he would receive from the Sheriff when he brought back three-quarters of the crop. After all, there was no way that Clarence could fight him and his six men.

He got off his horse and walked over to the barn. The watching crowd held their breath as they saw him glance inside and nod to himself. He only had to look closer and he would notice that the centre of the barn had an area of fresh sawdust covering new wooden floorboards. If he looked more closely at these he would find that they covered the old ice pit.

But he didn't. He was in too much of a hurry to get started. He strode up to the front door of the manor house and rapped loudly.

'Open up, Clarence! My men and I are here to "help" you gather your wheat!' He emphasised the word "help" sarcastically and laughed at his own wit.

Clarence looked at the group of outlaws and then went to answer the door. He had rehearsed what he was going to say well to avoid making the sergeant suspicious.

He opened the heavy oak door and bowed slightly to the man. 'We've been expecting you. Please help me. I can't afford to give you three-quarters of my wheat. I know you must have something for your "help", but couldn't you just take one-quarter? I have found extra people today so that your men need not do so much work.'

He opened the door wider and indicated Robin and his outlaws, who came forward, each carrying a big knife for cutting the wheat and a pitchfork for gathering it together.

The man's reaction was exactly what they had hoped for. He threw his head back and laughed. It wasn't a happy laugh. It was loud and cruel.

'Dear Clarence,' he said. 'I'm pleased to see that you have lined up extra help but if you think I shall allow you to keep more of the crop because of it, you are very much mistaken. These children may make it quicker for the wheat to be gathered in – but they certainly don't scare me or my men.'

He turned to relate this to his men and they all began laughing. Still playing his part well, Clarence looked disappointed.

Within a few minutes Clarence's men and the outlaws were hard at work in the fields. Each took a section of the field and began cutting the wheat and gathering it into neat piles. Meanwhile, the soldiers sat in front of the barn playing cards and making jokes about what they would do with the bonus

26

which the Sheriff would pay them for the wheat.

Robin scowled furiously at the lazy thieves sitting so arrogantly, but he contented himself with thinking of the plan they had up their sleeves.

After about an hour of working, large piles of wheat stood next to each worker. It was time for the next stage of the plan to be put into action. Robin looked across at Little John and nodded. Then they walked together back to the barn, passing the thieves as they went inside and collected the old hay cart. Walking round the field, they went first to Friar Tuck, then to Marian, and threw the piles of wheat into the cart. Next they went over to young William. He had deliberately been given the section of the field furthest from the barn and furthest from the eyes of the soldiers. Being careful to block their vision with the cart, Robin and Little John threw William's wheat on to the cart. Then they lifted the young boy in after it and quickly threw the wheat over him before continuing around the field.

After a few minutes the cart was piled high with wheat, and buried inside and well out of sight was William. He heard the soldiers joking as the cart went past them at the entrance to the barn.

'Good. One cart load down, many more to go,' one of them shouted. 'Hurry up and dump it inside the barn and get back to work. We can't sit around all day waiting for our share of the profits.'

They were soon inside the barn and away from the gaze of the soldiers. Quickly, Robin and Little John pulled the barn door shut behind them. Then they unloaded the wheat and lifted William off the cart. Pulling back the floorboards, the three of them looked down into the huge ice pit.

'Plenty of room to hide a harvest, I think,' said Robin, laughing. 'Now it's up to you to get on with it, William. We'd better get back to work before we're missed.'

As soon as Robin and Little John left, William began throwing the wheat into the pit and before long the whole cartload lay in one corner of it. Over the next few hours the two older boys returned several times with more cartloads of wheat. Each time, the soldiers greeted the new cartload happily and each time Robin and Little John closed the barn doors so that nothing inside could be seen.

By lunchtime the whole field had been cleared of wheat. The last cartload had been left with William to throw into the pit. All the outlaws needed to do now was to put the final part of their plan into action.

The man in charge of the soldiers, however, had other ideas.

'Right,' he called. 'Glad to be of help. Now we'll just go into the barn and take our three-quarters and then we'll be on our way.'

His men stood up from their card-playing and turned towards the barn doors. Robin caught Clarence's terrified glance. They needed more time for their plan to work. They had assumed that the soldiers would sit around a little longer and eat before leaving. If they walked into the barn now, they would soon find out what William had been doing.

Suddenly, Friar Tuck staggered from the manor house kitchen carrying a large barrel of wine.

'Won't you join us in a drink of celebration?' he called. 'It's only right that we have a few moments of enjoyment after our efforts.'

There was no way that the Sheriff's men were going to refuse the wine. Reluctantly, their leader let go of the barn door and went to join his men.

William, from inside the barn, had heard every word. He knew that he now had at least half an hour to finish his work. Throwing the last of the wheat into the pit, he noticed that it almost completely filled it. Clarence's fortune would be saved by a harvest this big and it was up to him to keep it hidden.

He took up the floor boards and slotted them into a groove made a little way down inside the hole. Then he grabbed a spade and began filling the remaining hole with a pile of mud, which had been left there for the job. When he had finished, the wheat lay safe inside the hole and a layer of mud covered the top of it. It was now safe from everything – including fire!

Taking a flint out of his pocket, William struck it several times. At last he managed to get a small flame. Carefully, he set light to a small bundle of hay, which had been left in the far corner of the barn.

The Fire and The Festival

'FIRE! FIRE!'
William came running into the kitchen, screaming at the top of his voice.

'The barn's on fire! All the wheat's inside! Come quickly and help!'

From his shouting nobody would guess that William had just spent the last five minutes calmly watching the fire take hold of the old barn. Then, when he was sure that it was too late to put it out, he had run into the kitchen to raise the alarm.

The soldiers threw down their goblets and rushed outside. On seeing the blazing barn they dashed back into the kitchen to fetch water.

'Grab anything that will hold water!' yelled the man in charge. 'And put that fire out!'

The men grabbed buckets, jugs, vases, tankards and dishes, but just as William had planned, it was too little too late. There was no way the barn fire could be put out.

Robin and the outlaws and Clarence all took care to look sad and disappointed. In no time the barn had completely burnt down and all that was left was a smouldering heap of ash.

With a roar the man in charge threw down the vase in his hand and it smashed on the stone floor.

'We've wasted enough time on this wretched farm!' he shouted. Then, looking straight at Clarence he said, 'My only satisfaction is that whatever I have lost, you have lost too!' With a wave of his arm he and his men strode out into the courtyard, mounted their horses and galloped away.

When they were safely out of sight, Robin, Michael and Little John ran to where the barn had been. Together they scooped out handfuls of mud until the wooden planks were exposed. Then Little John reached down into the hole and pulled out a bundle of wheat. He held it up for all to see.

'Fresh and dry,' he said, laughing. 'Completely undamaged.'

A cheer went up from the others. Above the noise Clarence spoke loudly.

'How can I ever thank you? You saved my harvest and with it you have saved my land. My father and I will be forever in your debt.'

'It's Little John and William you should thank in particular,' said Robin. 'It was Little John's idea and William's bravery in carrying it out, that really mattered.'

Everyone clapped and cheered again. Robin noticed Friar Tuck looking thoughtful.

'What is it, Friar? Are you not happy that we have beaten the Sheriff again?'

'Oh yes,' said Friar Tuck. 'But I was thinking that if Clarence really does want to thank us, I have one suggestion. It is always good to show appreciation to God by holding a harvest festival when the crops are safely gathered in.'

There were nods and murmurs of approval.

'If we were to hold a slightly extended harvest festival,' he continued, 'I think it would provide a very welcome treat for the younger children back at the camp. They really do miss village life and this would seem to be the perfect opportunity to ...'

'Say no more,' interrupted Clarence. 'That's a splendid idea. If you bring all the children over here two days from now, we'll show them the finest harvest festival ever. After all, without your help there would have been no harvest at all!'

Robin led a happy but tired group of outlaws back to the camp that afternoon and Anna and the other children were amazed to hear of their adventures. By bedtime they were all counting the hours until the harvest festival.

Robin and Friar Tuck had already discussed the dangers of taking the children out where the Sheriff's men could stumble across them but both agreed that it was a reasonable risk to take as it would give the children's spirits just the lift they needed.

'Look at young William,' laughed Robin. 'He's the hero of the day.'

William was surrounded by the younger children and over and over again he answered questions about how he had hidden inside the hay cart and how he had stored the wheat and started the fire. The air of excitement went on late into the night and no one got very much sleep.

At last the morning arrived and they were up and ready to go bright and early.

Robin gave everybody strict instructions

about what they must do if they came across any danger on the way. When he was convinced that they all knew exactly which signal meant to hide in the bushes, and which meant it was safe to come out again, he led them out of the secret camp and on to the forest path.

On the way, they hid on one occasion when Friar Tuck heard footsteps behind them. They were relieved when it turned out to be only a young farmer hurrying along the path towards the market, but nevertheless they took no chances and let him go on past them before continuing their journey.

After a little more than an hour of quick walking, they arrived at Clarence's estate and they all stopped and stared in awe. In the two days since they had left, Clarence had done a wonderful job. Flags and banners hung everywhere in the traditional style of a harvest festival.

Outside the manor house a long wooden table was laid with food of every kind and all around the table wheat had been woven into traditional ornaments. Some were in the shape of dolls and farm animals and others were woven together as huge decorations.

'He's certainly been very busy,' said Robin.

'It's wonderful,' exclaimed Marian. 'This is just what the children need, isn't it, Anna?'

Anna nodded. 'Look. In the fields there are games and tournaments already set out. And an archery area, Catherine.' She pointed to the three large targets.

There were courses set out for all kinds of races, and best of all, Robin could see that Clarence had marked out a jousting area. Clearly he was planning to put on a show for the children later.

'Jousting,' breathed William, looking at Robin with eyes sparkling. 'It's going to be fun!'

This would be a fun joust, Robin knew. An entertainment for the children. It involved men on horseback trying to knock each other off with huge metal poles called lances. Sometimes, though, men challenged each other to serious jousts when people were injured and lives were at stake.

After their long journey the children were keen to get started on the feast that Clarence had laid on. Robin was determined to be responsible, and before they could eat he insisted they made plans in case of danger.

'Where are the best places to put our look-outs?' he asked Clarence.

'Don't worry about that,' replied Clarence. 'This is a day for you all to enjoy yourselves. I have already placed lookouts in all the places they need to be. If anyone approaches whom we're not expecting you will hear a signal. My farmers' sons can make a sound that is just like a sheep. If anyone approaches you will hear so much baa-ing that you will think a whole flock has arrived!'

Robin smiled. 'That's very good planning,' he said. 'But where would we all hide if the alarm is raised?'

'Where else but in our old friend the ice pit!' said Clarence, laughing. 'We have taken just enough wheat out so that there is room for you all to climb in. Once the planks of wood and the mud are replaced nobody could find you.'

Robin was satisfied and relieved to have some of the responsibility taken off his shoulders. And so the feast began. Nobody could deny that the children were well looked after in the forest, but still this meal was the best they had eaten for months. There were huge hams, great slices of beef, and more chicken than they could ever eat. Fresh bread, cheeses and butter lay on gigantic plates – all surrounded by fresh fruit and salad.

Robin saw Marian approaching. 'The children are tucking in as if they haven't eaten for weeks,' he said.

She smiled, lighting up her lovely face.

'Oh Robin, bringing them out here for the day was definitely the right thing to do. Even when you're in hiding, there has to be a day out every once in a while.'

He felt his own face redden at the warmth of her praise and, to hide his embarrassment, he turned to Clarence.

'What else do you have lined up for us this afternoon?' he asked.

'I think you might enjoy the first thing,' Clarence replied. 'It's the archery contest. I believe that everyone expects you to win that one!'

'Not quite everyone,' shouted Catherine. 'I'm not too bad myself, you know.'

The girls all cheered at Catherine's challenge whilst the boys booed and hissed good naturedly. This was the signal for everyone to leave the table and for the farmers' wives to clear away the plates in case they had any unwelcome guests.

The fun and games were about to begin.

FUN and GAMES

As expected, it was a very close and exciting archery contest. Nobody else was really in the same league as Robin and Catherine, although Little John was not far behind. After everyone had shot five arrows, Robin and Catherine were joint leaders. Each had shot all five of their arrows into the yellow circle at the centre of the target. Little John had come third with three arrows in the yellow circle and two in the green circle just outside it. Marian had managed two in the green area and was pleased with that, her laughter ringing out across the fields as she handed her bow to the next contestant.

Catherine helped the younger children to have a go as the bows were large and the strings needed a lot of strength to pull back. Four-year-old Mary managed to get one of her

45

arrows to hit the edge of the target and she giggled and jumped up and down happily.

'So we're joint winners, five yellows each,' said Robin to Catherine.

'Not likely,' laughed Catherine. 'This time we really are going to see who the best archer is. I demand a shoot-off.'

Once again the girls cheered and the boys booed and hissed.

Robin quickly agreed. The rules were simple. The contestants drew straws and the person with the longest one was free to choose whether to go first or second. Then in the order agreed they would shoot one arrow each at the target. The person closest to the very centre would win.

Catherine drew the longest straw and happily said that she would go first. She took a long aim and then let the arrow go. Straight and true it flew towards the target and from the moment she let the string go she knew it was a perfect shot.

Sure enough the arrow landed right in the exact centre of the target. There was no way that Robin's shot could be any better. She turned to Robin and as a gesture of sympathy offered to shake hands but to her surprise he ignored her outstretched hand and instead picked up his own bow and took careful aim.

Further and further he pulled the string back until it seemed that he would snap the bow. At last, with a cry of effort, he let the arrow go.

Nobody who saw that arrow fired would ever forget it. It flew flat and hard, faster than any normal arrow. It flew straight towards the centre of the target – straight towards Catherine's arrow.

The crowd gasped, and held their breath.

Then to their amazement, it hit the very top of Catherine's arrow, but with the force that it had been fired, it didn't stay there. Instead it cut clean through the wooden shaft of Catherine's arrow, brushing it aside as if it was made of butter. A split second later, Catherine's arrow lay in two pieces on the ground whilst Robin's stuck proudly out from the centre of the target. It was an impossible shot – but it had won the archery contest for Robin.

Little John went forward to pick up the two pieces of Catherine's arrow and examine them closely. Then he looked back at the stunned crowd.

'Thank goodness you're on our side – and not the Sheriff's,' he said.

Everyone laughed and a crowd of cheering children surrounded Robin while Catherine accepted her defeat with a smile.

The races came next and Clarence had thought of an amazing variety. Young William won the obstacle race in which there were nets to climb over, barrels to crawl through and thin wooden planks to walk across. There was a sack race in which contestants had to pull a sack up to their waist and leap forwards. Eight-year-old Gwendoline showed that she was surprisingly good at this by jumping ahead of all the older boys and girls.

Finally there was a race called the egg and spoon race in which a fresh egg was balanced on a spoon and the children ran forward trying not to drop the egg. Every time an egg was dropped it smashed on to the ground and of course it wasn't long before all the broken eggs were being thrown around by the children.

There were so many different races that almost everyone won something. Even little Mary managed to win one junior race, with plenty of help from Clarence.

48

After all the excitement of the races the children were very tired and Clarence held up his hand for silence.

'Now, for your entertainment, ladies and gentlemen, we have a grand jousting contest.'

They all moved into the jousting area where he showed them his special surprise. First of all, two very big horses were led on to the track. One was black and wore a bright red coat under its saddle. The other was white and wore a bright blue coat.

The children gasped at how splendid the horses looked. They were even more amazed when Clarence and one of his farmers came out of the manor house dressed in full suits of armour. Each carried a huge metal lance more than twice their own height.

'This is the family armour,' said Clarence, proudly. 'I thought there was no point just storing it away, so we might as well show it off.'

Both men were then helped on to their horses, which was difficult because the armour was so heavy. When they were in their saddles their lances were passed up to them. They looked a fine sight. Robin felt very grateful to Clarence for all the effort he had put into entertaining the children.

Both riders charged up and down the track performing various tricks. Sometimes a ring was thrown in the air and one of them caught it on the end of their lance. Another time they charged towards each other and just as it seemed certain they would crash, one horse turned one way and the other turned the other way.

At last Clarence turned to the audience.

'Now for the big event,' he said. 'We are going to fight a proper jousting duel.'

He caught Robin's eye and the latter grinned, knowing that this duel had been well-rehearsed. The younger children laughed and shouted with excitement.

Both horses walked one hundred paces in the opposite direction to each other. Then they turned, paused for a moment, and then charged on a collision course.

There were gasps from the children but Robin noticed that just before the horsemen reached each other, they slowed down slightly. Then, just a fraction before they collided, both men pulled their lances away. To the younger children, however, it looked as if they had really struck one another with their lances, and when Clarence's opponent slowly slid from the saddle and fell to the ground, a great cheer rose up.

Clarence played his part to the full. He pulled his helmet open and turned to face the cheering children with one hand raised in victory. It was a great moment and everyone was having fun, forgetting temporarily their other worries.

'What a wonderful day we're having.'

Robin looked round to see Marian beside him again, but before he could answer, a loud noise came from the far corner of the field.

'Baa, baa, baa, baa ...'

On and on it went, as if a whole flock of sheep were running riot. Robin recognised it immediately. It was the signal from the look-outs that somebody was coming. There was no time to lose.

'Quick, everyone! Follow me, as quietly as you can,' called Robin.

He, Little John, Marian, Catherine, Friar Tuck, Anna and Michael rounded up all the younger children and led them to the old ice pit. The mud had been removed in case of such an emergency and Clarence removed the wooden planks within seconds. Then the scared children started climbing down on to the wheat. It was a tight squeeze, but at last everyone was inside.

Robin was last. Just as he was about to jump in he glanced over to the far corner of the field. Four men were riding towards them and he could just make out their shapes. There was something familiar about the one in front. It was the sergeant who had trapped and imprisoned him in Nottingham Castle a few weeks ago. A loyal follower of the Sheriff of Nottingham.

Robin was sure that the sergeant's arrival meant bad news for Clarence and he suddenly knew what he had to do. To everyone's surprise, he didn't join them in the ice pit but quickly put the planks of wood in place and brushed the mud and dirt over them, leaving just a small hole to let in air. Then he motioned to Clarence to get well away from the pit while he, with only a few seconds to spare, climbed up the trunk of a large tree.

Safe for the moment in its branches, Robin watched as the sergeant and his men stopped in front of Clarence. It was difficult for him to hear everything that was being said but he could just about follow the conversation. At first Clarence smiled at the sergeant and the sergeant smiled back. Both men spoke quietly for a few moments before the sergeant began to shout loudly.

'What a fool we have here, boys. What kind of idiot dresses up in armour to play children's games? It is either a fool or a coward who does that and from what I know of his stupid old father, I would bet he is both!'

Even from where he hid Robin could see Clarence reddening with anger. The sergeant had clearly insulted not just Clarence but his father as well. With family honour at stake Robin knew that Clarence would feel he had no choice but to challenge the sergeant to a duel. This time, though, it would be for real!

THE DUEL

6

Robin was horrified. Proper jousting was a very different matter to the pretend jousting that Clarence had shown the children. He knew that there was something very wrong with this challenge. The sergeant had clearly come looking for trouble and what's more, he was a proper soldier trained in fighting.

Clarence, on the other hand, was nobody's idea of a tough fighter. The sergeant was clearly up to something and Robin felt powerless to stop him. He watched helplessly as the men prepared for their duel. As Clarence was already in his armour, he waited whilst the sergeant dressed himself in the other suit of armour. Both men were then helped into the saddle and each was handed a long lance. Then Clarence's farmers led his horse to one end of the jousting track while the sergeant made his way to the other, surrounded by his men.

As Robin watched, he noticed one of the soldiers fitting what looked like a small rod just underneath the sergeant's saddle. It was on the left-hand side of the horse, the side which would pass nearest to Clarence's horse. What was it? What was it for? Robin was certain that the sergeant was not planning a fair fight. It was obvious that a lot of scheming had gone into this trickery.

At a signal from one of the sergeant's men, both horses set off towards each other. Robin watched, his heart in his mouth. This jousting was certainly nothing like the one which had been acted out for the children. Now each horse was galloping as fast as it could and each rider was clearly ready to do battle. There was a tension in the air such as Robin had never felt before. Clarence looked so different to the quiet young man whom he knew. For the first time, he looked like a real knight to Robin – a son that his father would have been proud of.

When the horses were just twenty paces apart, Robin saw the sergeant play his trick. Using his foot on the left side of his horse, he flicked out the rod. Now it clicked into place and Robin could see that it was a sharp iron spike, about two spans of a man's hand in length. The sergeant's leg hid the spike from view.

For Clarence's horse, though, it was a different matter. When they were only a few paces apart it got a perfect view of the spike and acted as any horse would, by turning sharply away.

The sudden turn ruined Clarence's aim and his lance passed harmlessly over the sergeant's head. From his viewpoint, Robin could see that the sergeant didn't even bother to aim his own lance at Clarence and he understood why. In the rules of jousting, if neither man is knocked off, the one who turns away is the loser. Clearly this had been the sergeant's plan for winning the duel, and what's more, within seconds the sergeant had clicked the spike back into place, flat against the saddle.

To Clarence it was a mystery why his horse had turned away, but he had no other choice than to accept defeat and, in the tradition of a gentleman, he rode towards the sergeant and offered to shake hands.

The sergeant, however, held his hand back. Instead, he shouted for all to hear.

'Do you think that I would shake hands with such a coward? Only the worst kind of coward runs away like that in a jousting duel. You would be a disgrace to your family if your father were not an even greater coward!'

Robin was beginning to understand what was happening. The sergeant was deliberately pushing Clarence towards a further duel, only this time he surely intended more than family honour to be at stake.

'I am no coward!' shouted Clarence, just as Robin had expected he would. 'And my father most certainly isn't one either. I won't let you call him a coward. On his behalf I challenge you to another duel – and this time I shall not fail to knock you off your horse.'

The sergeant laughed loudly, trying to provoke Clarence's anger even more.

'You have had your chance to defend your family honour – and you ran away,' he shouted. 'Why should I joust again with a coward? I have better things to do than listen to the empty threats of a man too scared to fight. Anyway, I've already won the duel, and that is that.'

Clarence's anger was totally out of control. For several seconds he said nothing and then, in a low voice which Robin had never heard before, he spat out another challenge.

'You will fight me,' he hissed. 'I know that it's too much to expect one of the Sheriff's sergeants to fight just for honour, but you will fight me again because you are a greedy thief. This time I will offer you a prize that you can't resist.'

The sergeant listened, a contemptuous smile on his face.

'If you win,' went on Clarence, 'I will give you half the harvest from my land this year and every year in the future. If I win, I will satisfy my family honour.'

The sergeant nodded his agreement and his men applauded. Robin was horrified. So this had been a cleverly thought out plan and exactly what the sergeant had been aiming for all along.

Clarence's face was white with anger as he turned his horse back along the jousting track. Robin knew exactly what thoughts must be running through his mind. He had lovingly looked after his father's land these past five years and now he risked losing half of it in the next few minutes.

But he didn't know that the odds were against him. The sergeant intended pulling the same trick with the metal spike and was confident of a win. Robin could not let this happen. Only he could stop Clarence from losing his land. Whatever the danger to himself, he had to warn Clarence.

Without waiting a moment longer, Robin jumped down from the tree and ran towards the jousting track, yelling at the top of his voice.

'Clarence, stop!'

Clarence turned in his saddle.

'It's not a fair duel,' shouted Robin. 'The sergeant has a spike attached to his saddle and when he flicks it out your horse turns away. Don't let him take your land!'

Within seconds chaos broke out. One of Clarence's men, who was near the sergeant moved forward to look at the saddle.

'It's true!' he shouted, grabbing hold of the spike. 'The sergeant has been cheating.'

The sergeant kicked the man out of the way and then glared at the figure who had raised the alarm. For a moment he frowned, unable to think who it was, and then he recognised the boy who had stolen the Sheriff's treasure. The boy whom he had imprisoned in Nottingham Castle and who had escaped and made them all look like fools.

His face turned purple with rage and he bellowed, in a voice loud enough to be heard by the children hiding in the ice pit.

'Robin Hood! You may have saved this fool from losing his land, but you will wish you had not interfered. This time we have you and this time we will not let you get away. You have meddled for the last time, Robin Hood!'

ROBIN'S LEAP

7

For a moment nobody moved. Robin glanced at Clarence. He could see both gratitude and fear in his friend's eyes. Robin had risked his life to save Clarence's family heritage. Now he was out in the open and hopelessly out-numbered, and what's more, the sergeant and his men were on horseback. He had no doubt that the outlaws in the ice pit could hear what was happening and he prayed that they stayed where they were.

Now it was his move. In a split second he made a decision to dash for it. He raced towards the far corner of the field where the hedge that surrounded it was highest, not having much idea of how he could escape but with some kind of plan forming in his mind as he ran. If only he could get as far as the hedge before the soldiers reached him, he was sure he could find a hole to squeeze through. The hedge at this end of the field was too high for a horseman to jump over and if they dismounted and chased him on foot, he was convinced he could get away from them. After all, he was younger and fitter – and he was running for his life!

Robin chanced a look round. He knew he had gained a few paces on them at the start, but now they were drawing closer and closer with every stride. He was still some way from the hedge when he realised it was useless. Two of the men rode straight past him and positioned themselves along the hedge, facing him. They were taking no chances this time. The others spaced out on his other side.

He was surrounded.

'We have you now, Robin,' shouted the sergeant, galloping up and reining in to a stop. He was grinning and confident. He and his men approached Robin, tightening the circle. It would only be a matter of seconds before one of them jumped down and grabbed him. He was about to surrender.

Then from the corner of his eye, he saw a flash of light racing across the field, moving so fast that at first he couldn't make out what it was. Then he realised. It was Clarence! Clarence, still wearing his armour and holding his jousting lance. The sunlight flashed off his armour as he galloped.

The sergeant had his back to him and it was only at the last minute that one of his men saw Clarence and shouted a warning. It was too late for the sergeant to react. Clarence was charging at full speed towards them.

'I don't remember us ever agreeing to end our little jousting competition,' he shouted from a few paces away. With that, he swung his lance and hit the sergeant a mighty blow which knocked him to the ground where he rolled around, yelling in pain.

Then, to Robin's surprise, Clarence half fell off his black horse in a crash of armour.

'Quick!' he shouted. 'Take my horse. It's the fastest one I've ever had.'

Robin saw his chance. With one leap he was on to the horse's back, turning swiftly and racing back up the field in the opposite direction.

Again, Robin had a few paces start over the sergeant's men but this time it was a fair race as they were all on horseback. The trouble was that again Robin had no definite plan of escape. He only knew that he had to get out of the field. The hedges were too high to jump,

69

so it had to be through the main gate. At least then he might have a chance of losing the soldiers in the forest.

He stared at the gateway, still a long way ahead. It was blocked! The gateway was completely blocked! What was it? He squinted, staring hard at the object. Someone was pushing a huge old hay cart across the opening. It must be one of Clarence's farmers. What did the fool think he was doing? That had been his only escape route and now it would be impossible to get through.

Robin thought hard. It wasn't like Clarence's men to trap him like this. They were good and loyal farmers who would be on his side, not the Sheriff's. Then, suddenly, he remembered a conversation long ago with Clarence. He had always been particularly proud of this black horse that Robin was now riding. He boasted about it. How fast it could run. How amazingly high it could jump. According to Clarence, there was no horse in Nottinghamshire that could jump higher or further than his favourite black horse.

That was it! The farmer wasn't blocking him in but giving him a chance to go where other horses couldn't follow! Robin rode faster and

70

faster straight towards the cart. He could sense that the riders behind him had slowed down. They would not expect their horses to attempt this impossible jump, or his either. Any minute now his horse would stall at the cart and throw him off and they would capture him.

But Robin rode on. 'Don't let me down now,' he whispered in the horse's ear.

The horse galloped on, ears forward, concentrating. All Robin could do was to hang on. The horse was going to try and that was all he could ask. It knew exactly where to launch itself from so as to go as far and as high as possible. They were almost on top of the cart when he felt it gathering itself under him, its powerful hindquarters ready to spring them into the air.

As the front legs rose in the air, Robin was terrified. He gripped with his knees, leaned forward and prayed. It seemed that they were in the air for a lifetime. At last the horse's hooves thudded down on to firm ground. They had made it! They had jumped clear over the hay cart. It had been an unbelievable jump.

Robin glanced round to see the sergeant's men jumping off their horses to push the hay cart out of the way, but he had gained valuable time and there was no way they could catch up with him now. He raced as fast as he could towards the thickest part of the forest and then risked another glance behind him. The sergeant's men were distant figures, only just leaving the field now. Robin couldn't resist waving cheekily at them. Then he jumped off the horse and patted its rump.

'Thank you,' he said. 'I owe you my life. Now you must go back to your master.'

Then he ran into the dark forest where he could travel faster on foot. Nobody knew the forest better than Robin and it was only a matter of time before he would be home and able to relax. He grinned to himself as he pictured the sergeant's anger which would be vented upon his poor soldiers. They would ride away defeated and Clarence could then open up the ice pit and release the outlaws. They would all be wondering what had happened and Robin was sure that Clarence would enjoy describing his escape!

Clarence certainly did! The outlaws were upset to hear how he had been tricked in the jousting contest, but they cheered and laughed when they heard how Clarence had knocked the sergeant off his horse. They gasped in wonder as he told them about the impossible jump which Robin had made in his escape, thanks to Clarence's black horse, which had returned home and now snuffled contentedly as they patted its neck.

Marian could not stop herself from kissing Clarence on the cheek. 'What a brave man you are,' she said.

Clarence blushed at the kiss and the kind words and was quite relieved when Friar Tuck took charge and spoke to the children.

'It makes no sense to stay here too long. You never know who may come back and cause trouble. Everybody please get ready; it's a long walk.'

'You must take some food with you,' said Clarence. 'Come into the kitchen.'

They filled their mouths and their pockets and had something to drink. Then, after thanking Clarence again, they set off.

'Why don't I walk ahead of the group?' suggested Little John. 'Then if I see anyone I can run back and give you plenty of time to hide.'

'Good idea,' said Friar Tuck. 'The younger children are tired out after the day's excitement and struggling to stay awake, but we must carry on. We won't be safe until we reach the camp.'

Friar Tuck relaxed a little and Little John moved on ahead, looking carefully around each corner as he came to it. Then, when he saw that it was clear, he ran on to the next corner.

After a few minutes he reached the wide river which was one of the most dangerous parts of the journey. The path led along the bank of the river until it reached a narrow wooden bridge which must be crossed to get back to the camp.

As he began to run quickly across it, Little John had the strangest feeling that he was being watched, and just at the moment when he reached the middle, a figure appeared at the far end. He was a big rough-looking man and from his clothes looked like one of the Sheriff's men. Little John turned around and saw that he was in real trouble. At the other end of the bridge was another one of the

Sheriff's men, and this one looked even bigger and tougher than his friend did!

LittLe John Raises the ALarm

8

The two men walked towards Little John while he desperately tried to think of ways to escape. So the sergeant must have been suspicious. He must have realised that Robin may not be travelling alone and he had posted lookouts, and now, thought Little John, he wouldn't be far away.

Big and strong as Little John was, he was no match for two trained soldiers, and they clearly thought so too, for as they approached he could see that they were quite relaxed.

The one in front spoke first.

'Ah, Robin's tall friend. The one they call Little John, I believe.' He looked Little John up and down and laughed. 'And I can see why. You are aptly named, but now your luck has run out. Our sergeant has outwitted you and you are our prisoner now, and something tells me that you are not alone. I'm sure your friends are not far behind.'

The soldier behind spoke.

'Yes. The sergeant was right. He told us that if we spread out across the forest, one of us would spot you soon enough. Now all we have to do is raise the alarm and all the sergeant's men will be here within minutes.'

Both men laughed and began moving towards Little John. He would soon be their prisoner. He had to do something, and not just for himself, but for the others. Unless he could somehow warn them, they would walk straight into a trap.

Then he had an idea.

'You may catch us but you will never find Robin. After all, he has more brains in his little finger than you have in your entire bodies.'

As he had expected, an angry frown appeared on the face of the soldier in front of him and he rushed towards Little John, pulling his fist back and aiming a mighty punch at him. Little John ducked. The soldier lost his balance and fell forward, his fist connecting with the stomach of the soldier who had been behind. The punch was a good one and the soldier fell to the ground clutching his stomach, while the one who had thrown the punch fell on top of him in a heap.

Now Little John had to act quickly. He had no doubt that the punched man would be out of action for a while, but the other was already struggling to his feet. Little John reached down and grabbed the back of his collar with one hand and his belt with the other. Then, with a huge cry of effort, he pulled the man up off the ground and on to the barrier along the edge of the bridge. With a final push, he threw him over and into the water below.

There was no time to lose now. The soldier in the river was already splashing furiously towards the bank, and the other one would soon recover from his pain. He must go and warn the others before the alarm was raised. Jumping over the fallen soldier, he raced back across the bridge, but just as he reached the path he heard the sound of a hunting horn and knew it must be the sergeant's men. Clearly the alarm had been raised and within minutes the forest would be swarming with men searching for the children.

Little John ran on and soon reached the tired-looking children.

'Quick! You must hide!' he shouted. 'The sergeant's men are everywhere.'

They looked around helplessly. This was the

worst possible place to hide. On one side of the path was nothing more than thin bushes and on the other was the open river. They would never be able to run into the deeper part of the forest and here there wasn't anywhere for one person to hide, let alone over thirty!

'Quick! Run anywhere,' shouted Friar Tuck. 'At least that way some of you might escape.'

There was a panic as children looked around, wide-eyed, hesitant, afraid, not knowing where to go.

'No, wait!' said Little John. 'There's no point in just running. I believe there is still somewhere we can all hide. Follow me!'

To everyone's surprise, he did not lead them back towards the forest but scrambled over the rough ground towards the river.

'What are you thinking of?' asked Marian. 'We can't all swim across.'

Little John shook his head, leading them away from the fast-flowing part of the river and towards a bend which was quite over-grown with rushes and weeds.

'This is where we'll hide,' he said.

'There are too many of us for the rushes to hide us all,' Anna protested.

Again Little John shook his head. 'No, the rushes won't hide us. We'll be hiding under the water, not above it!'

THE DUNGEON

'**R**ight everybody, watch!' said Little
John. 'There's only time to show you
this once and then you'll all have to do your
best to copy.' He picked out a tall, thick reed
nearby and neatly pulled a long straw free and
held it up.

'Look at the end of it,' he said. 'It's hollow.
That means air comes through it, so you can
breathe through it.'

Little John took the reed and placed it in his
mouth. Bending it so that the end pointed
upwards, he waded into the river. Then, still
with the reed in his mouth, he lowered
himself below the surface and moved down
slowly until there was no sign of him. All that
could be seen was the reed sticking upwards,
looking exactly like the thousands of other
reeds all around.

'It's the perfect hiding place!' said Marian.

'But I'm not so sure ...' began Catherine, indicating the children. 'Some of them are so little. It's very dangerous. Someone may drown.'

'It's their only chance,' said Anna, taking her gently by the arm. 'Come on, let's help them find their straws.'

The three women quickly helped the younger children and, one by one, they lowered themselves into the river, holding on to each other beneath the water so as to stay together. Above the water, all that could be seen was more than thirty reeds sticking up in the air.

After a few minutes in the cold, dark river, Little John carefully raised his head, just above the surface. All around, the sergeant's men were searching the path and the land beyond. Not a bush or tree was being ignored, as they became ever more frustrated.

Quickly, Little John ducked his head beneath the surface again. Despite the cold and darkness he smiled to himself. They had done it again. They had outwitted the Sheriff, the sergeant and all their men! All they had to do now was wait.

For young William the wait seemed to go on

forever. He could feel a sneeze building up inside his nose. He held his breath. Sometimes you could stop a sneeze by holding your breath. Please, please stop, he told himself desperately. But the sneeze built up and up until at last it erupted with a great whoosh.

The noise of the sneeze broke the silence of the river bank. One of the sergeant's men spun round and spotted William, who had had to raise his head above the water.

'Look!' shouted the soldier. 'There's one of them in the river! The idiot is trying to swim away from us!'

For everybody else it was lucky that William's sneeze had blown the reed straight out of his mouth. At least when the soldiers spotted him, there was nothing to show that he had been hiding, or that there was anyone else nearby. Hopefully, they would think that he'd been split up from the rest.

William waded towards the bank so as not to give the others away, and seconds later was grabbed by two strong men and dragged up the river bank. There he stood, shivering in front of the sergeant, little rivulets of water running off his green outfit and forming puddles on the ground.

'Where is Robin?' thundered the sergeant. 'Tell us now or it will be worse for you.'

'I d-d-don't kn-n-ow,' stammered William, shivering from cold. 'They all ran off in the other direction when they heard you coming. I fell over and got lost. By the time I got up they had gone, so I hid in the tree and then tried to swim away when I thought you were going to find me.'

The sergeant glared at him and William met his gaze bravely.

'Take this wretch out of my sight!' shouted the sergeant. 'He's an idiot and a friend of Robin Hood. There's only one place to take him. The dungeons of Nottingham Castle. We'll soon see what he really knows about Robin.'

William's heart thudded as he was dragged away by the two soldiers. The dungeons! No one had ever escaped from there! They were dark and damp and underground. There were no windows and they would have guards on the doors. Rescuing him would be impossible.

Only Little John saw poor William being led away. He had raised his head just above the surface of the water and gazed sadly at the boy, who looked so small between those two big men. The dungeons were no place for anyone, let alone one so young.

When he was sure that the soldiers had left, Little John gave the signal for everyone to come up. Then he told them what had happened.

It was a quiet, wet and subdued group who made their way back to the secret camp where Robin was waiting anxiously for them. He was delighted at their safe return, until he heard about William.

All that evening there were long discussions and arguments about William. Despite their tiredness, some of the younger children wanted to go straight to the castle to try and rescue him.

'He's in the dungeons,' Friar Tuck explained, again and again. 'They're underground and have no windows and only one heavy metal door.'

'Besides,' said Little John. 'The Sheriff will be expecting us and will have posted extra guards.'

Robin felt wretched and Marian came up and laid a hand on his arm.

'It's not your fault, Robin,' she said.

'We should never have let the children out,'

he said. 'They were safe here. It was my fault, for wanting to fight the Sheriff.'

She shook her head. 'You couldn't just stand by and watch him carry out his cruel and unfair laws,' she said. 'None of us can. You are our leader and we will always follow you.'

He looked at her and then looked away, reddening. Sometimes he couldn't think of anything to say at all.

The misery of the outlaw's camp, however, was nothing compared to how poor William felt that night. Already cold and wet from the river, he had been forced to walk all the way to Nottingham Castle. His hands were tied together in front of him and then the rope was attached to the sergeant's horse. When the horse moved quickly, William had no choice but to run after it and by the time they reached the castle gate, he was exhausted and almost glad to see it.

This feeling didn't last long. As soon as they were inside he was handed over to the jailer and his assistant. The jailer was a filthy old man with hardly any teeth, who looked as if he lived underground. His assistant was a huge man who never spoke. When he opened his mouth William saw that he had no tongue.

'Don't worry about Jim,' laughed the jailer, seeing William's shocked expression. 'He won't say a word to you. He can't. He hasn't spoken for twenty years, ever since the Sheriff had his tongue cut out for lying.'

William shuddered, and not only from the cold. The jailer opened a huge iron door and pushed him through. Then the three of them descended a dark spiral staircase, the jailer's flickering candle making dancing shadows on the wet walls, green with mould. The cold air smelt stale and musty.

'How do you like your new home?' asked the jailer, holding the candle aloft so that William could see the large room with the stone floor, walls and ceiling. The jailer was laughing, a high wheezing sound echoing round the walls. His stinking breath reached William's nostrils and he felt sick.

'You might as well make yourself at home,' wheezed the jailer. 'I reckon you'll be here for a long time.'

William followed the jailer into the bare

room. Or at least he thought it was bare. He soon found that he was horribly wrong. Up on the wall, well above head height, two iron rings hung from the wall.

The jailer held up the candle to illuminate them. 'I hope you won't get too bored here on your own,' he said. 'But in case you do, we have a few toys which might interest you. These rings may help loosen your tongue. They don't look much, I know, but hang up there for a few hours and the pain is terrible.' He chuckled again. 'And if that's not enough, we have our old friend the rack.'

William heard a grunt behind him and turned round. The noise had come from the assistant jailer. He must be laughing, too. He was pointing to a far corner of the cell where William could just make out the shape of a long wooden bench with ropes and straps attached.

The Sheriff's rack was legendary and William never wanted to see it close up. Everyone knew that even the bravest men had cracked when strapped to the rack. Your arms were pulled one way and your legs the other, and the pain was terrible. You felt as if you would snap in half.

'Anyway,' said the jailer, 'we can't stay down here talking to you all night. Sleep well! The Sheriff will be down in the morning to ask you a few questions about Robin Hood.'

William watched as the jailer and his assistant climbed back up the stairway, carrying the candle with them. Then he heard the clang of the iron door shutting behind them, and he was all alone in the dark.

william meets the sheriff

As soon as the door banged shut, William burst into tears. He had been determined not to cry when the sergeant had caught him, or even in front of the jailer, but now he was alone there was no reason to hold back. Things really looked bad for him. The Sheriff was going to question him about Robin and if he didn't tell them what they wanted to hear, they would torture him on the rack!

Just then he heard a noise, and stopped crying and listened. The door at the top of the stairs had opened again, and William could see a flickering light and the shape of a big man placing a tray down on the top step. It was the jailer's assistant.

The door banged shut again and William groped forward and carefully climbed the steps towards the small light. The man had left a stub of candle, some bread and some water.

Suddenly William felt a little better. At least

he wouldn't have to spend the night in total darkness and he would be able to take the edge off his hunger. So Jim was not so bad. At least he might just have one friend who wanted to help.

William did not sleep well that night. For one thing he was cold; the only covering he had was a damp, threadbare scrap of blanket. At last, morning showed as a thin strip of daylight through a slit high up in the wall.

William looked round. It was not a bad dream. He really was here, locked up in the dungeon, awaiting questioning from the Sheriff.

For a long time nothing happened. He had no way of knowing what time of day it was, except from his hunger, having long since finished his bread and water. Then a key scraped in the lock, the iron door burst open and the jailer came down the iron staircase, followed by four soldiers. Two of them carried a huge oak chair with a red cushion on it.

Finally, they were followed by a tall, well-dressed man with a beard. William recognised him from a visit to Edwinstowe a few months before. Even at that time the Sheriff of Nottingham had scared him. Now, as a prisoner in his dungeon, William was terrified.

Nobody said anything until the Sheriff was sitting comfortably on his chair.

'There is one simple rule today,' he said, looking at William. 'If you tell lies to us, we will be forced to hurt you. We will not hesitate to use the rack to make you tell us the truth.' He looked around at his four soldiers. 'My men and I will find that very amusing, even if it is a little tiring. *You* will not. Do you understand me?'

'Yes,' said William, in a voice that didn't seem like his own.

'Good,' replied the Sheriff. 'Now, why don't you start by telling me who you are and how you know this Robin Hood thief.'

William was ready for this. He had spent hours during the night thinking about what he may be asked. To him, it was clear that there was no point in refusing to speak. They had everything on their side and would be able to make him tell them what they wanted ... eventually. He had to appear to be helping them, and the only thing he wouldn't tell the truth about was the location of the secret camp.

William spoke clearly and politely to the Sheriff. He told him who the other outlaws were and of all their adventures so far, which was little more than the Sheriff already knew. None of it would help him catch Robin and the others.

Then came the question he had been dreading.

'And where do you all live?'

'We live in the forest,' answered William, truthfully. Then, a little less truthfully, he added. 'Robin leads us from one camping place to the other. We never spend more than two nights in one place, in case anyone discovers us.'

'Put him on the rack!' bellowed the Sheriff in a hard, cold voice.

Several hands grabbed William and he struggled, but it was no good. He was picked up and put on top of the wooden rack. He lay there, shaking with fear, the hard wood digging into his back. Then his hands were pulled above his head and tied firmly to the top of the rack, and his feet equally firmly tied to the bottom of the rack. Within seconds he was fully stretched out.

'Now,' said the Sheriff. 'You see this wheel?' He pointed to a huge wheel on the side of the rack, which the jailer and Jim were holding tightly. 'When I give the order they will turn the wheel. Then the rope will pull both your hands and your feet. At first it will feel strange, but as you become more stretched it will be very painful. Do I make myself clear?'

William said nothing. Tears came into his eyes and he angrily closed them so that the Sheriff would not see him crying.

'Now, do you have anything else to tell me?' asked the Sheriff.

William shook his head.

'All right. Turn the wheel.'

There was a creaking sound as they began to turn the wheel. Still William said nothing. He was ready for the worst now.

Then, to his astonishment, the Sheriff shouted again.

'Stop! He was obviously telling the truth, otherwise he would have told us by now. We have better things to do with our time than stretching stupid young boys!'

William let out a sigh of relief as he was lifted from the rack. He hadn't told the Sheriff anything that mattered. He watched as the Sheriff climbed the spiral staircase, but just before the iron door he stopped and turned.

'They say Robin Hood is good with the bow and arrow,' he said. 'Is that true?'

William was far too relieved not to answer such a harmless question. Happily, he spoke up.

'Oh yes. Robin is a fine archer. He can hit the very centre of the target whenever he likes. What's more, Catherine is almost as good. Only the other day she almost beat him. Her arrow was in the very centre of the target but he beat her by cutting straight through her arrow with his own.'

The Sheriff considered this for a moment and then shouted.

'Give him bread and water. We may have a use for him soon, but until then he can stay in the dungeon.'

The iron door clanged shut behind them and William was left alone to wonder whether or not he had just given the Sheriff some information which could be used against Robin.

The sheriff's challenge

It was Anna who found one of the posters the next morning. She had been collecting nuts and berries just outside the camp when she had heard the soldier approaching, so she had hidden and watched while he nailed the poster to the tree.

As soon as he had gone, she tore it down, then read it over and over again before taking it into the camp.

A meeting was immediately called among the older outlaws. As they sat under one of the huge trees, Robin spread the poster out on the ground in front of them.

'Good old William,' he said. 'It's clear from this that he has not told the Sheriff where the camp is, otherwise there would be no need for such a challenge.'

'What is it?' asked Little John, craning to read over Robin's shoulder.

'It's called the Silver Arrow Challenge,' said

Robin. 'And it says, "The Sheriff of Nottingham hearby challenges Robin Hood to a Silver Arrow Challenge. The rules are that Robin and one of his outlaws shall compete against two members of the Sheriff's household. The teams shall draw lots to decide who will shoot first. Following this, the first team shall shoot their two arrows. Then the second team will shoot their arrows. Whoever has the arrows closest to the centre of the target at the end wins the contest.

' "If Robin Hood wins, he shall win the freedom of young William. He and his fellow outlaw shall also be free to leave. They shall also take with them the prize of a solid silver arrow.

' "If the Sheriff's team wins, William will stay in the dungeon forever and Robin and his fellow outlaw will join him." '

'When is it to take place?' asked Friar Tuck.

'Noon on Friday,' answered Robin. 'In front of Nottingham Castle.'

'Only two days from now,' said Marian, looking at Robin with a worried frown on her face. 'At least we know that William is alive and well at this moment, since he is being offered as a prize.'

'But will the Sheriff keep his word?' asked Little John. 'Or is it just a trap to catch you, Robin?'

'I don't think so,' said Friar Tuck. 'The Sheriff is an evil man, but he wouldn't go back on things said in public.'

'You think not?' said Catherine. 'You think too well of people, Friar Tuck.'

Robin shook his head. 'If there is any trickery involved, it is in the way the contest will be organised. I'm sure it is a trap, yet I can't see how we can ignore the challenge.'

'It's obvious that you and Catherine will have to go and win the contest,' said Michael. 'The way you both shot the other day, I don't see how you can lose.'

Robin shook his head again. 'Catherine will not be going. It will be no place for a girl, especially if we lose.'

Catherine struggled to her feet, looking down indignantly at Robin. 'I *am* going!' she said. 'I can shoot almost as well as you, so I can take the consequences if we lose.'

Robin opened his mouth to argue.

'That's it!' said Marian, suddenly. 'I've just worked out what's bothering me. One day you and Catherine shoot so well in a competition and the next the Sheriff challenges you to a contest. William must have told him about it, and now he's relying on you feeling confident enough to take up the challenge.'

'We have no reason not to be confident,' said Catherine.

Little John thought for a moment. Then he said.

'What if the Sheriff plans to fix it so that you have to shoot first?'

'That shouldn't be a problem,' said Catherine. 'I don't think he has anyone working for him good enough to perform the same trick as Robin managed!'

'If I know the Sheriff at all,' said Michael. 'I would guess that's exactly where his trickery lies. I'll wager he has an expert archer all lined up who knows that he will be shooting last. He's probably practising shooting through the tops of other arrows right now.'

For a long while nobody spoke. They were sure that they had worked out the Sheriff's plan. However, when it came to rescuing William none of it helped. They had no choice but to take up the challenge. If only they could think of a way of beating the Sheriff at his own game.

Suddenly, Michael shouted. 'Get me an arrow. I have an idea!'

Catherine passed him an arrow and Michael jumped up and walked off towards the far corner of the camp where he had a sheltered area he used as a workshop.

'Well I'm glad someone has an idea,' sighed Robin, getting to his feet. 'So far we've managed to beat the Sheriff, but this time I'm not so sure, and one of our children's lives is at stake.'

They soon began preparing food for themselves and the children, and it was about an hour later when Michael returned and handed the arrow back to Catherine. She weighed it in her hand and examined it closely.

'It looks the same,' she said. 'But it feels slightly different.'

When Michael told them why, they gasped in astonishment. Even Robin smiled for the first time since William's capture. It was the perfect answer to any trickery the Sheriff was planning. Now they could really take up the challenge with confidence.

All the next day Robin and Catherine practised their archery. Again and again they shot

arrows into the target. It took them a while to
adapt to the heavier arrows after Michael's
work on them, but by the late afternoon they
were firing them perfectly. Almost without
fail, each arrow was shot into the centre of the
target.

As the day progressed everybody became
nervous. It was agreed that it would be far too
dangerous for anybody else to go apart from
Robin and Catherine. The Sheriff would have
to let those two pass freely, but he would
happily imprison anyone else spotted there.
Nobody liked the idea of just waiting without
knowing what was going on, but they all
accepted that they had no choice. All except
Marian, that is.

Marian could not bear to be far away from
Robin at this time of danger and she decided
that, whatever the risk to herself, she would
make her own way to the castle to watch the
Silver Arrow contest.

the silver arrow

The next day Robin and Catherine set off early. In his pocket, Robin carried the small leather purse which contained the lucky four-leafed clover which Old Alfred had given to him and which he always carried in times of need. Today, of all days, he hoped it would bring him luck.

As they arrived at Nottingham Castle the sight made them gasp out loud.

'Look at all the people,' exclaimed Robin. 'There must be hundreds.'

Already waiting for them on a stage was the Sheriff of Nottingham. In front of him, mounted on a plaque, was a solid silver arrow, flashing brilliantly as the sun caught its smooth burnished shaft and head.

'There's William,' said Catherine, pointing to a small boy at the foot of the stage. She gathered up her skirts and started running forward, shouting, with Robin close behind.

'William!' Catherine and Robin both hugged him and Robin was shocked to see how thin the boy had become in just a few days. William managed a smile.

'What a touching scene,' said a voice behind them, and instantly the crowd fell silent. 'It's so good to have your company at last,' said the Sheriff. 'I think it will be many years before you leave us again. Do you and this girl really think that you can beat me?' He turned to sneer at Catherine, and then to the crowd of onlookers.

'He brings a wench as his fellow contestant,' he shouted. 'There must indeed be a scarcity of good archers amongst the outlaws!'

The crowd roared with laughter and jeered and whistled until the Sheriff held up his hand for silence and turned to call his men over.

'May I introduce my team. You have met my sergeant, I believe?'

The sergeant glared angrily at Robin.

'And this is a new member of my staff – Sir Wilber Blackhand. He is my new Archer in Chief. You may know him better as the Archery Champion of all England!'

A gasp went up from the crowd and Robin looked at Catherine. Sir Wilber Blackhand was well-known to everyone with an interest in archery, but it was the first Robin knew of his being on the Sheriff's staff.

'May I ask,' said Robin, 'When Sir Wilber was appointed to your staff?'

'Why, several days ago,' smiled the Sheriff. 'He was appointed on a salary of one hundred gold sovereigns a year.'

So this was the Sheriff's trick, and no doubt he was planning to make sure that Sir Wilber had the final shot in the contest.

'Don't worry,' whispered Robin to Catherine. 'As long as we shoot as well as we can, he can't beat us.'

Catherine smiled bravely back, knowing that Robin was not as confident as he sounded.

'Let the contest begin!' the Sheriff shouted. 'We shall draw lots for who will shoot first.'

A man approached, carrying a velvet bag in one hand and two wooden balls in the other. One ball was marked with the number one and the other with the number two.

This was the moment of truth, thought Robin. This was the time when the Sheriff would cheat. He watched closely as the man placed the balls into the velvet bag, but not quite quickly enough to deceive Robin.

Adeptly and skilfully, the man had slipped the number two ball up his sleeve and replaced it with another number one. If he hadn't been expecting it, Robin would never have spotted what was going on. Now, smiling to himself, he pulled a ball out of the bag. Sure enough it was a number one.

'You shoot first!' shouted the Sheriff, triumphantly.

Robin nodded his head to Catherine, who carefully fitted her arrow into her bowstring and raised it to shoulder height. She was nervous, he could see, shaking slightly, but as she took aim her nerves went and she shot the arrow straight and true, right into the centre of the target.

A small cheer went up from the crowd, until the Sheriff's glare silenced them.

Now it was Robin's turn. He, too, fitted his arrow and raised the bow. He had become used to the slightly heavier arrow which Michael had given him. Then he pulled back the bowstring and arrow, took aim, closed one eye, and lined up the target with the shaft of the arrow.

With a whoosh the arrow shot away and the bow-string twanged. It seemed a long moment as the arrow flew through the air and then thudded into the target next to Catherine's arrow, quivering a little. His was the perfect one.

Their part of the contest was done. Robin stole a glance at the Sheriff and thought he looked a little nervous. The only way for his man to win now was for his arrow to hit the very head of his own and cut through it like a knife through butter.

First was the sergeant's shot. It was quite good, but some distance from Catherine's and Robin's. Now was the moment that everyone had been waiting for. A hush descended over the crowd. It was as if everyone were holding their breath.

Sir Wilber lifted his huge bow and pulled the string back as far as it would go, until it was clear that he would be firing with great force. In his sights was the head of Robin's arrow. Cooly and calmly he let the bow-string go.

The arrow flew faster than any of the other three. It whipped through the air, straight and true, the perfect shot in every way.

'CLANG!'

The noise rang out over the silent field and a gasp went up from the crowd. What had happened? People near the front craned forward to see.

Robin's arrow still stuck out from the centre of the target. Sir Wilber's, however, lay on the ground.

The Sheriff was speechless. It was impossible that an arrow shot with the force of Sir Wilber's should just bounce off like that. Sir Wilber strode forward to the target and pulled out Robin's arrow, examining it closely, weighing it in his hand. Then he broke it across his knee and looked at it again.

'It has been fitted with a metal cap,' he shouted to the Sheriff. 'Impossible to split.'

Robin nodded. 'Of course, we had to get used to the heavier arrows,' he said, 'but we had all day yesterday to practise.'

A great cheer went up from the crowd. They clapped and stamped their feet and surged forward to congratulate Robin and Catherine. Robin quickly snatched the silver arrow with one hand and William with the other and the three of them rushed off the stage and into the crowd. The Sheriff would not publicly go back on his word and already they felt safer, surrounded by hundreds of people, but they would only feel really safe when they were back at the camp.

With an arm round William's shoulders and

Catherine by his side, he hurried towards the path leading to the forest. The crowd pushed and milled around them, wanting to shake hands, to pat them on the back. Beating the Sheriff was a triumph for them all.

At last, as they were getting closer to the forest, he saw a sight that made him freeze. Standing on the edge of the crowd, under a tree, was Marian. So she had not been able to resist coming to watch. It was a stupid risk but he could understand how she had felt. He would have done the same.

At that moment, there was a shout from the stage.

'Over there! The girl under the tree. She's one of them. Get her!'

Things moved quickly from then on. At first it seemed that none of the soldiers would be able to get through the crowds of people to reach Marian. Then one bright young soldier jumped on his horse and raced around the edge of the crowd, stopping just long enough to sweep Marian off her feet and on to the saddle in front of him.

It all happened so quickly that even the crowd could not react in time to save her. Robin had a clear view of Marian from where he stood. He had the bow slung on his back. If only he had an arrow.

But he did! Just as the horseman was turning to gallop back to the stage, Robin fitted the heavy silver arrow into the bowstring, aimed and let it fly.

The arrow was not meant for firing. It was heavy and could not fly a long distance. Fortunately the target was not too far away and it struck exactly where Robin intended, ripping through the sleeve of the soldier's shirt and thudding into the tree behind, pinning him to it.

Marian was ready and took this chance to wriggle free and urge the horse forward, leaving the soldier to fall to the ground as his shirt sleeve ripped. Robin, William and Catherine dashed forward and jumped up, on to the horse behind Marian.

As they raced into the forest Robin looked behind. The crowd now completely filled the path. It would be impossible for anyone to chase them. On the stage he could just make out the Sheriff shaking his fist in anger.

Robin grinned. They had lost the silver arrow but they had won their freedom.